TREASON OF THE BLOOD

TREASON OF THE BLOOD

by Marion Zimmer Bradley

TREASON OF THE BLOOD

Every night, as darkness folded over the Castello di Speranza, the little Contessa, Teresa, descended to gloat over her prisoner. There were formalities to this visit, each stylized as the motions of some pagan priest celebrating some high and ancient ritual before the altar. First she dismissed all of her servants, even the deaf—mute Rondo who obeyed her as a trained dog. Then, each night bruising her frail hands anew on the steel, she drew the bolts of her chamber and fastened the locks of earn casement. If some mythical observer could have hidden behind the arras he would have seen a strange thing; into each metal bolt, roughly and painfully scratched by hands unused to such labor, the sign of the cross had been inscribed.

Then she knelt for a moment before the oaken priedieu, clasping her fingers about her beads; mere habit now, for she had long ceased to pray. The mirror at the far end of the chamber gave back her reflection dimly, a shadow pattern in black and white; the black coils of her hair netted with thin lace, the close black of a mourning gown crossed by the clasped fingers of white hands on ivory beads, her face—drawn to the whiteness of bone, of alabaster-brushed with black silken brows.

A face made for softness and for love, but hard now and cruel, the eyes level with hate, the soft mouth drawn to a thin white line. A saint, transformed by the double lashes of grief and sworn revenge into a fiend from the pit.

Rising and laying aside her beads, the Contessa lifted the lid of a carven chest, and took a three—thonged whip of braided leather. At the end of each thong, bits of razor—steel had been fixed; the leather was blackened and the bits of steel dulled with a dull brownish—red stain. She touched her fingertips to the steel and drew them back quickly; the sharp steel had drawn her blood.

She shrugged, disregarding the pain. In the leather grip of the quirt, crudely cut by an inexpert knife, was again the sign of the cross.

There was no answering creak as she drew back the bolt of the secret panel. This door was kept oiled and in perfect repair. A taper held high in one hand, she descended the stairs as noiselessly as her own shadow, her trailing skirts sweeping aside fresh cobwebs and sending small spiders scurrying into the cracks of the stone.

TREASON OF THE BLOOD

The brackish smell of stagnant underground pools came up to meet her. There had been a time when her delicate nostrils had shuddered at this smell, but that time was long past. She herself hardly realized how much she had changed from the young girl, afraid of every shadow, her frail fingers bleeding from the struggle with the then—rusted bolt, who had first come down these steps in despair and terror.

She paused and sighed. "Why do I come?" she asked almost aloud, and tike an echo cast back from the dank depths there was a whisper and a sigh, "Come."

Two turns of the winding stair and she came into an arched corridor, lighted with dim moonlight filtering down long shafts built centuries ago. The passageway was lined with remnants of a grimmer day; the rusted bars of a pulley still suggesting the strappado, a crisscross of bars like a hard couch, the grim green—bronze stare of an Iron Maiden. The Contessa barely gazed at these things which once had made her shudder; now they seemed familiar friends. She toyed, indeed, with a moment's thought they could be put in order before she turned the final twist in the passage, where a steel grating reared from stone floor to arched ceiling. Taking the great key from the chatelaine at her belt, the Contessa unlocked the grating and passed through.

"Good evening, Contessa," said the man chained to the wall.

The Contessa bowed her head. "And to you a good evening, messire, she said in her melodious voice, whose modulation was so deep a habit that even the transformation of maiden to fiend could not alter it.

She surveyed the man before her; his arms encased in cuffs of iron secured to the wall by long chains that passed through a ringbolt there. His legs too were locked in anklets of steel joined by a chain. A tattered white shirt and dark—stained leather riding breeches were all his clothing, yet, as he bowed, his fair hair caught the gleam of the taper and the dancing shadow, on the stone wall seemed to reflect wide wings.

The woman, standing carefully beyond the furthest reach of the chain, let her eyes linger on the features, thin, sharp and subtly sensual. As he raised his head again, his eyes, blazing with some strange spark, crossed hers. He shuddered as if with some terrible pain. The long look was almost like a lover's glance. Again the Contessa was shaken by the curious beauty of the chained man. Beauty? A strange word, yet beauty it was, the beauty of some restless caged eagle, beating its wings with the fierce despair and agony of its inhuman hunger. But his glance fell first, though when he spoke his voice held a lilting mockery.

"You are beautiful this evening, madonna," he said, "I regret that I may not kiss your hand."

A spasm of indefinable emotion seemed to convulse her face. "So," she said abruptly, "kiss if you will," and extended her slender fingers, bruised and bleeding, to him. It was a mocking gesture, but he seized her hand in his and bent low over it, touching his lips to the hand. Then, abruptly, he struggled as if sudden madness possessed him, his chained hands crushing over her wrist, bringing them up avidly to his lips.

With a single swift gesture she brought up the whip and, wrenching her other hand free, lashed out with a single brutal blow. He flinched momentarily and in that instant she was beyond his reach again, her eyes flaming.

"I had forgotten," she taunted, "it is full moon and you—hunger!"

He stood slumped in his chains, not deigning to answer her mockery. At last he said, quietly, "Aye, full moon again. Are not your dreams evil, madonna?"

She shuddered as if to ward off the memory, but said, "I count myself lucky if you can do no more harm than this—to send me evil dreams!" A spasm of disgust twisted her mouth. Suddenly she stepped back and caught up the whip again.

"Angelo, Count Fioresi," she cried in a ringing voice, "You have fed on your last victim—vampire!" She laughed aloud.

"Three months have I kept you in chains and watched your strength diminish and your evil hunger grow!"

Suddenly he strained wildly against the chains, but the spasm was feeble and soon he fell back exhausted, leaning against the wall and sagging.

"Once you could have burst those chains," she said, smiling in cruel triumph, "had I not carved the cross into each bracelet! Now even ordinary chains would hold you, I think!" He propped himself up on his hands.

"Madonna," he said in a low voice, "my life is at your mercy; you might end it at your pleasure.

TREASON OF THE BLOOD

None could blame you, if you sought my death. But why do you find pleasure in tormenting me?"

"Need you ask?" she cried in a high anguished voice—the last remnant of the young girl she had been three scant months ago. "You, who came to this castle as my suitor, beguiling my father by posing as the grandson of his oldest friend? How often he spoke of you, saying he felt, when he was in your company, that the friend of his youth had returned from the dead? He did not know how true he spoke!"

The Count shook his head.

"No," he said wearily. "If you must tell again that old sad tale, tell it truly. That is but old wives telling, that such as I return from death. We do not die, but live many times the span of mortal men, unless accident cuts off our life—or, or, we are barred too long from our other source of life."

Her convulsed face seemed to waver in the dim light.

"Be it so then. Your old friend, my father, sickened and died, then Rico my brother, of a wasting sickness. Last of all Cassilda, the sister who had mothered me when I was left motherless, was laid in unhallowed Earth—still you sought to wed me."

"Madonna, you call me a fiend—"

"Can you deny it?" she cried. "Can you claim to be man, you who have touched neither food nor drink in these months since I brought you here?"

"I have admitted I am not a man of your sort," he said, his head bowed. "My race is far older than yours, Madonna, perhaps made before your own God gave dominion to your kind. Like some beasts, we live—when we have passed youth—only by the blood of living things. Till my thirtieth year, I thought myself as other men. Yet I did not kill your kin, Contessa. And if I had; if I had? Your eldest brother Stefano was slain in a duel with the lord of Monteno, yet Monteno's kin are honored guests here in Castello di Speranzo. I did not know." He seemed suddenly to writhe in pain—"I did not know, death was already in your kinfolk when I came here."

"You lie!" she cried out, and the lash whistled in the air as it caught the man across face and chest. He cried out hoarsely and the fiend smile crossed the girl's face.

"It gives me joy to know that you can suffer!" she cried. "Suffer as I suffered!"

The whiplash had drawn blood; she looked at the crimson drops with a strange gloating smile.

"Have a care, Lady," said Angelo, Count Fioresi, softly. "I sought the blood of men so that I might not die; you have come to seek it for pleasure."

She raised the whip again, then lowered it.

"Why can I not seek your death?" she cried. "Why did I not kill you then? What can I not rid God's sweet earth of such a thing as you?"

"And why are your dreams so evil?" he asked softly, "and why was it that once you loved me, Madonna? Your God has forbidden revenge to his faithful. Why could you not slay me, and leave me to his vengeance and hell—or to his mercy?"

She turned suddenly and fled down the passage and up the winding stairs. Her footsteps made crisp echoes in the night. And Angelo, Count Fioresi, man, monster, vampire, whatever he was, dropped his face into his hands and wept.

The Contessa flung her windows wide, shivering as the night wind blew the dungeon stench from her gown; she would have knelt, but the words of the vampire burned in her heart; God has forbidden revenge.

What have I become? she asked herself, almost in wonder. She lay down in her great bed, but she feared to sleep, so great was the encompassing horror of the dreams that visited her. It was some evil spell of the vampire she held chained, she told herself; yet so great was the terror at the nights of full moon that she dared not close her eyes. She lay there recalling how she had first trapped the evil thing in man's form which lay now in her dungeon.

When first he came to them he had been ever at hand. She thought it was Cassilda's hand he sought, for her sister was both older and more beautiful; yet he showed to Cassilda only a curious courteous kindliness.

It was the kindliness which she could not now reconcile with the horrors. When her father, then her brother had died, she had wept, "I am ill—fated; you cannot want me now." He had smiled and said, "Perhaps, when you are my wife, evil fortune will weary of following you."

But it seemed as if some evil spell lay on them all in those days, for there were deaths all through the village, as if some mysterious sickness plagued them. At last even Cassilda died, though the castle's priest, Father Milo, hid away her body from Teresa.

Angelo had come to her that day where she wept near the chapel—aye, she now, recalled, he had never stopped within the chapel doors here—his fair and beautiful face wrung with what had seemed to be honest compassion. Was it truly hell—black hypocrisy?

"Teresa, Teresa, I cannot bear to see you so alone!"

Now she wondered; what, indeed, would have happened, had she succumbed to his pleas? Could he indeed have come within the chapel? Her cross—signs had held him fast; could he have wedded her indeed?

Would, she not, indeed, have accomplished her purpose by binding him fast in Sacrament. . . ?

Father Milo, drawn and quivering with his own terror, had drawn her into the chapel that night, and signed her with the cross, then bidden her sit on his bench while he stood before her, his face taut with pain and horror. At first she had hardly listened to his rambling tale of strange deaths in the village, the marks found on the throat of her father and brother, the hint of some more dreadful horror surrounding Cassilda's death. Only slowly and incredulously did she realize what he was telling her—that these deaths were the work of a vampire!

"But this is only wicked superstition," she cried in protest, and he shook his head.

"No, it is the devil's work, done by one in league with that same devil!" Father Milo replied, his face drawn and white. Slowly, word by word, he had convinced her. Even then she had never more than half believed the dreadful tales he had told—that the Count had been seen to fly in the form of a bat from the windows of the old tower, that a holy woman of the village had smelled grave clothes and the musk of the coffin when he passed by; but when at last she believed, she had knelt before the priest, a passion of rage and terror surging up in her heart.

"What can be done?" and Father Milo answered slowly:

"The creature must die."

"Death alone would not serve!" she cried out in anguish, her face as white as her mourning veil. "I remember—I remember the night before she died, Cassilda came to my bedside and wept; and I—I did not know, why!"

Father Milo laid his hand on her head. "Bear what I must tell you now, with courage, my daughter. Cassilda died by her own hand, for fear of that same fate."

TREASON OF THE BLOOD

Teresa cried out in pain. "Then death alone cannot serve this monster! He must suffer—suffer as I and mine have suffered!"

"Revenge belongs to God alone," the priest rebuked.

"I know not for certain, but I have heard that these monstrous creatures of the devil—cannot truly die, but live on in their coffins, rising to seek the blood of living things. Daughter, I must travel to Rome, and seek dispensation to deal with this—this thing, so that we may be rid of him forever." "You must go tonight."

"But first we must make all secure," replied the priest, "So that he cannot harm you nor destroy you as he has done to your kin. Be watchful, but show no change in your manner, so that he will not suspect we know him for what he is. Then, when I return, we can destroy him and send him into true death back to his coffin for God in his infinite mercy to punish or pardon."

Teresa covered her face with her hands. "A thing from the grave and I had loved him!" she whispered. "God's mercy? I would see him burn forever in hell!"

The priest crossed himself, shaking his head sadly. "It grieves me that you speak such evil words," he said in rebuke. "Can you set limits on the mercy of God?"

"For that devil, yes!"

"Yet a great saint said once to Satan's self, daughter: 'to thee also I may promise God's mercy, when thou prayest for it.' Think you, Teresa; the Count Fioresi is a valiant soldier and a gallant courtier. He has borne this devil's curse many years, and for him this must be true hell, cast out of God's sight. Can you deny that the merciful God might one day pardon him?"

"If I thought this," she cried out passionately, "then would I find a way to keep him ever from that pardon—to make him live and suffer as me and mine!"

The priest had answered simply, "You are overwrought, and small wonder. Pray God to forgive your thoughtless words." He gave her his hand to rise. "I must go tonight; come now to your room, where we must make all safe."

His hands then had cut the sign of the cross into each door and window, and he had sprinkled them with holy water. He had left the main door for last, but as he turned to it Teresa felt a sudden, stifling terror. Even to save herself from death she could not endure to be shut in by spells, even holy spells.

"This I will seal myself with my crucifix when I am within," she said, and as she spoke, her plan leaped full—formed into her heart.

"Perhaps it is better so," he said thoughtfully. He drew from his robes a small vial. "Give him this in his wine," he said, "and God forgive us, daughter, but at least it will send him to the first death. When I return from Rome we will deal with the vampire, with stake and fire." Reverently he gave her a rosary. "This was blessed by a great Saint and is an heirloom of my family. It will keep him from rising from the dead until I come again." He laid his hand on her head in blessing. "And mark," he added severely, "forget these wicked thoughts of revenge! I command you, on peril of your soul's health, pray for the soul of this lost sheep of God; pray for the soul of Angelo Fioresi." But the words had fallen on a hard heart. She bowed her head, but cried out inside,

"Never!"

With her own hands she prepared food and drink for the first stage of the priest's journey; but as she bade him farewell and his palfrey ambled away, she had turned away with the first cruel smile, crushing the little vial in her hand. "But you will not return," she murmured, "and vengeance will be *mine*!"

Then, turning from the door, she met the smiling eyes of Count Angelo, and forced herself to smile and give him her hand to kiss.

"Why has the priest left us?"

"To secure permission for our marriage," she replied steadily.

"Then we are alone here?" he drew her close, smiling.

"May his journey be swift!"

But a curious frown had touched his forehead, and Teresa quailed and shrank from his kiss. "Not now!"

She lay awake that night, feeling like the chained goat staked out to draw the prowling mountain lion, the pale light from the open door lying across her face, waiting for the step and shadow, as of black wings across her door. She clasped the cross in terror, thinking; it is true, then, that the vampire moves like cat or ghost on noiseless feet.

Slowly the shadow bent till the full lips touched her throat, then, as if she feigned waking, she murmured, "Angelo?"

"Love—"

"Wait," she whispered, clutching the cross in her hand, "the door is ajar."

"Surely not," he whispered, turning, but with a scurry of step she reached it, slammed it to, and jammed the bolt together with the crucifix. "Now," she cried, white as her nightgown, "let me see if you can leave as you came, Angelo, Count Fioresi—fiend, monster, murderer— vampire!" She rushed at him, holding the light aloft. He whirled like a beast at the death, making a dash at the sealed windows, the other door, in vain. She said hi a voice that shook, "I never more than half believed, till now. It seemed a monstrous lie, but true, then!"

The Count stretched his hands toward her and she raised the cross to ward him away, but although she had expected him to rush at her, bent on murder, he did not stir. "Teresa," he implored, "it is not what you think. I beg—I implore you, hear me before it is too late." But in her wrath and fury she would not listen. She caught up the whip and rushed at him, raining blows on his face and shoulders. He cried out and with one swift movement wrenched the lash from her hands and cast it on the carpet.

"Have a care, lady," he said in a low, voice, "I know many things you know not. And I tell you, Teresa, at this moment you stand in peril more deadly than mine. Will you hear me—hear me but a moment, for the sake of the father who ties dead?"

Hear *you*, monster, murderer, grave—ghoul?" she cried, and a bleak smile crossed his face.

"The old tale that I rise from a coffin of death? No, Lady, I have never known death, yet. Nor do I want to die, yet. But if you kill me now, you pass into peril, so hear me first." He strode toward her again, as if he would seize her and compel her to listen, but she snatched up the crucifix from the prie—dieu and held it before her. He flinched away and she gloated, "So that much superstition is true?" He cowered, his lifted arm covering his face.

"True in part, Teresa; I cannot harm you while you bear that symbol of your faith, that sign that you are under God's protection. Yet for the last time I beg you—"

"Would you beguile me with words?" she cried. Crucifix in hand, she raised the whip and brought it down across his cowering form. He retreated a step and she followed, the lash rising and falling.

"So you can bleed and suffer?" she cried in triumph.

"Even as yourself," he muttered, and slumped to his knees: Warding herself with the cross, Teresa wielded the lash, savoring each dull crack and the thin lines of blood that gradually crisscrossed his body. At last she stood gasping above him; he lay senseless and bloody at her feet. With wary glances, fearing his faint was feigned, Teresa ran to the chest and dragged the heavy chains thence. Her own frail fingers had scratched the cross in each bracelet with her diamond ring. Then she summoned Rondo, the deaf—mute, and with his help she dragged the Count down the long stairs and, shivering, locked the chains to the dungeon wall. Then, sick with horror and replete with the satisfaction of her first plan of revenge, she fell almost senseless on her bed.

"Throw the windows wide," die motioned to Rondo, "I am fainting!"

When he had left she slept, but her dreams were evil. She seemed to rise and pass like a silent wraith from the castle, and confused horrors of blood and dying faces wandered in her mind. She woke to discover that she had walked in her sleep and lay half—in, half—out of the leaded casements.

Has he bewitched me? she wondered, as she fell across her bed in the growing daylight and slept.

She woke at dusk and descended, shuddering, into the crypt; but her fear was somehow soothed by seeing her enemy in chains. There she began the custom of descending each evening into the crypt . . .

As the days passed this began to absorb her more and more, so that she lived only for the moments when she came before the chained man, looked into his fierce eyes like a caged falcon, and when his pleas grew too disturbing, silenced them with the cruel lash into which she had now cut the cross so that he could not wrench it away.

The evil dreams still tormented her. The spell seemed to seize all the castle, for some of her servants fled, and others came to her with a tale of deaths in the village, but she brushed them aside like buzzing flies.

The maker of deaths is safely chained below, she thought; they cannot now ascribe them to supernatural visits, nor lay all deaths to such a cause! She was impatient and cruel with them, longing only for the moment when she would descend to gloat over her prisoner, then return to sleep the sleep of dead exhaustion.

The people of the village murmured because Father Milo did not return, and sent old women to her to beg that she should find another priest. "Would you command me?" she shouted, pacing the floor, and when the delegation had fled, she stared at herself in horror in the glass; they will think I am mad!

So three moons waxed and waned, bringing little change. Then came a night when Angelo barely stirred when she spoke to him, but lay seemingly senseless in the straw and chains.

At last he opened his eyes and murmured, "Gloat your fill at my despair, madonna. The end comes. But I see you passing further and further into peril. For your own sake I beg you; end this."

"Why," she mocked, "the devil was sick, the devil a monk would be! Shall I set you as priest in Father Milo's chapel?"

"I am no monster of cruelty," he said, "though I cannot blame you for thinking me so. Yet, Teresa, I am safely chained here. Why, then, the deaths of your people?" She shrugged callously. "Such folk are always dying. Am I responsible for them, bodies or souls?"

The chained creature gave her a curious calculating look. "Once you would not have spoken so. Once you were gentle and pious."

"And if I am a fiend from hell, who but yourself made me so?"

Almost he laughed. "No, no, you have guarded yourself from me, but have you not made yourself a fiend?"

"Silence," she shrieked. "Silence!" She brought down the whip full across his face, and, with a terrible cry he fell, blood breaking from his broken lips.

She let the whip fall, and knelt beside him. "He spoke truly; the end is near," she thought.

"Here let him lie forever."

The crucifix she still wore swayed back and forth, casting a strange shadow on her prisoner, and a random thought touched her: I have had my revenge. It is not too late to put aside my hate and do as Father Milo bid me; put an end to his sufferings and convey him to God's mercy. I need but strike him through the heart. He has said that he cannot rise from the dead. Even so I can pray for him the prayers for the dead, doing penance. Then will I, too, return to God's mercy. And Angelo—Angelo will pass to the dust he should long have been, and his soul settle for his crimes before God.

She had the strange sense that the dungeon was crowded with watching, waiting spirits; it was as if she stood at some crossroads waiting for a victim to be hanged or pardoned, and the victim was herself. She could cast aside hate, and seek mercy, or—Her lips curled in a smile of terrible cruelty. Never, never could she forego the pleasure she had found hi this! No, let him surfer, let him suffer forever! Who had need of God's forgiveness? There were many outside God's domain!

"So it is too late," he said. She shrank back, but moving inexorably he sat up, gripped her roughly and burst the chains from his hands, then from his ankles.

Teresa shrieked aloud, cowering back and starting to her feet. She tripped over the fallen lash and fell to the stones and Angelo, rising, strode to her and stood over her.

"I would have saved you," he said at last. "Think, Teresa, of your evil dreams. Had they not begun before ever I came to Castello Speranza? Long years ago, one of the women of the Fioresi married into the Speranza clan; and I knew that one at least of your kin would be—of the full blood of my folk. Had it been Rico, I would have taken him as esquire in my service, to guard and protect him. I—I would have saved you," he said almost inaudibly, "guarded you as a thing more precious than my life. I watched over you, kept you safe, guarded you in innocence of what you were, though I came too late to save your father—"

She shrieked in horror as the words filtered through her brain, but he went on remorselessly.

"When Rico met his death, I could bear it no longer, and in desperation, seeking only to guard you, I made it known to Cassilda. I—I did not know she would slay herself with the horror. I thought only that together we might guard you, till I could bring you safely to knowledge of what you were. You could have come to accept it—not as a thing of terror, but simply another kind of life; a different nature living harmlessly by its own laws. No, I did not slay your kin," he said. "I have lived so for two hundred years. Since the first year when I first learned what I was, no man has—died from my touch; I know how to—take life—and harm them no more than a leech's blood—letting.

TREASON OF THE BLOOD

I am neither evil nor cruel, madonna, because I live as I must."

He bent over her. She recoiled, mad with fear, and thrust the crucifix at him.

"No," he said gently, taking her shoulders hi his hands, "it will not protect you now." He went on, almost sadly: "I was reared to fear it; it was instilled into my inmost heart and brain, that I might never touch one who called sincerely on God's mercy. While you were still ignorant of what you were, Teresa, while you were sincerely pious in your faith, I could not pass through the symbol of your sincere belief. And the cross which you carved on my chains, thinking when you did so that you would protect others from my evil was a barrier to me. But now you have grown evil. You have rejected the teachings of your faith. You cannot call now upon your God for protection. The cross is now, to you, only an empty symbol, and it will not hold me."

He ripped the crucifix from her throat, gazed on it sadly and laid it aside.

"Perhaps I never had a soul," he said wearily, "but you, Teresa, cast yours away. You are too much monster even to live among my people."

The last thing the Contessa ever saw was his face, torn with pain, descending into a crimson blur into which she fell like death.

Hours later villagers gathered to watch the Castello di Speranza crash down in flames, and none marked the quiet, scarred man who rode silently into the forest, bowed as if in long agony, crouched in his saddle with grief and pain. He never looked back at the rising flame, but rode with head bowed over the neck of his horse and muttered again and again, "Teresa! Teresa! Teresa!"